W9-BQJ-012

FIGMENT

JOURNEY INTO IMAGINATION, VOLUME 1

ABDO Spotlight · Disney KINGDOMS · MARVEL

ABDOPUBLISHING.COM

Reinforced library bound edition published in 2016 by Spotlight,
a division of ABDO, PO Box 398166, Minneapolis, Minnesota 55439.
Spotlight produces high-quality reinforced library bound editions for
schools and libraries. Published by agreement with Marvel Characters, Inc.

Printed in the United States of America, North Mankato, Minnesota.
092015
012016

 THIS BOOK CONTAINS
RECYCLED MATERIALS

MARVEL
marvelkids.com
© 2016 MARVEL

Elements based on Figment © Disney.

CATALOGING-IN-PUBLICATION DATA

Zub, Jim.
 Figment : journey into imagination / writer, Jim Zub ; artist, Filipe Andrade
and John Tyler Christopher. -- Reinforced library bound edition.
   p. cm. (Figment : journey into imagination)
"Marvel."
Summary: Dive into a steampunk fantasy story exploring the never-before-
revealed origin of the inventor known as Dreamfinder, and how one little
spark of inspiration created a dragon called Figment.
ISBN 978-1-61479-445-5 (vol. 1) -- ISBN 978-1-61479-446-2 (vol. 2) -- ISBN
978-1-61479-447-9 (vol. 3) -- ISBN 978-1-61479-448-6 (vol. 4) -- ISBN 978-1-
61479-449-3 (vol. 5)
1. Figment (Fictitious character)--Juvenile fiction. 2. Dragons--Juvenile
fiction. 3. Adventure and adventures--Juvenile fiction. 4. Graphic novels-
-Juvenile fiction. I. Andrade, Filipe, illustrator. II. Christopher, John Tyler,
illustrator. III. Title.
741.5--dc23

2015955126

Spotlight
A Division of ABDO
abdopublishing.com

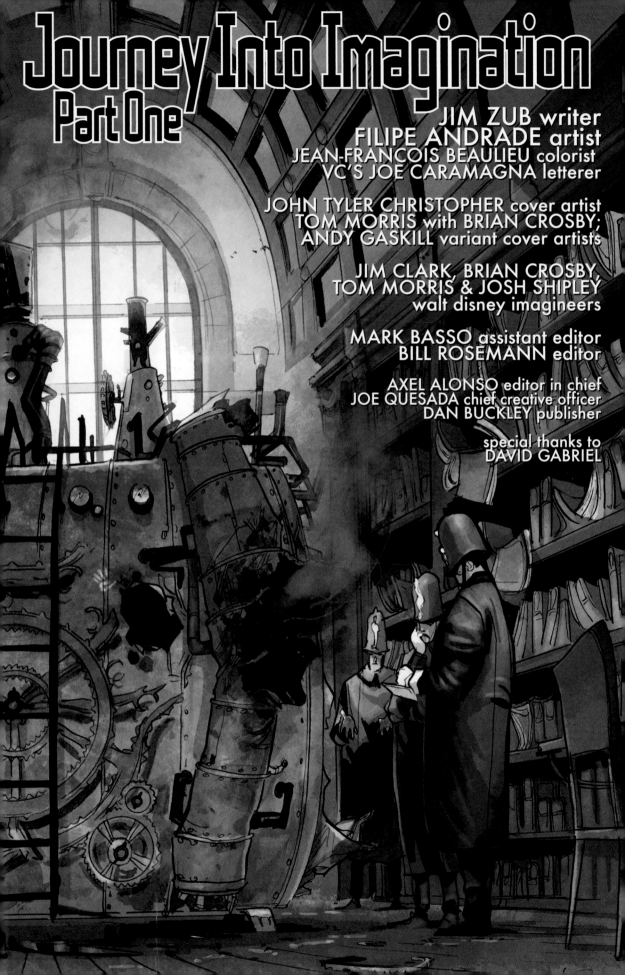

Journey Into Imagination
Part One

JIM ZUB writer
FILIPE ANDRADE artist
JEAN-FRANCOIS BEAULIEU colorist
VC'S JOE CARAMAGNA letterer

JOHN TYLER CHRISTOPHER cover artist
TOM MORRIS with BRIAN CROSBY;
ANDY GASKILL variant cover artists

JIM CLARK, BRIAN CROSBY,
TOM MORRIS & JOSH SHIPLEY
walt disney imagineers

MARK BASSO assistant editor
BILL ROSEMANN editor

AXEL ALONSO editor in chief
JOE QUESADA chief creative officer
DAN BUCKLEY publisher

special thanks to
DAVID GABRIEL

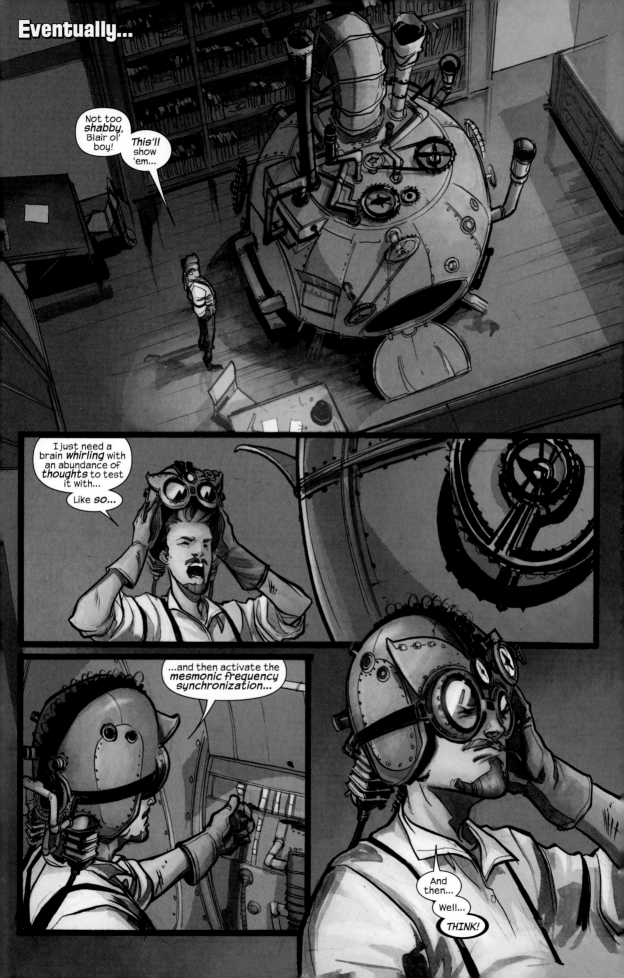

Day 1.

Some people see the world as it *is*.

Day 2.

They believe the environment around them is *static, immutable...*

Day 3.

...and that *setbacks* are a sign they should *settle* for what they have.

Day 4.

I prefer to think of the world as it *could* be.

Day 5.

It's a *journey* to create something *bigger* and *better*.

Day 6.

If I don't try, I'll never know how *big* it could be.

Day 7.

Is it ready?

I... I think so... *Pull* the *switch!*

KA- CHUNK

Hmmm... *That's* not good.

I don't think it's the *machine.*

It's *you...* You just have to use your *imagination!*

What?! That's exactly what I *am* doing!

You've just gotta see it in your head!

Find the same spot in your mind where you found *me!*

Don't tell me how to do my *job!* I don't need childish *daydreams,* Figment...

...I need something *bigger!* I *can't* fail! It *has* to work!

I...I'll just *reverse* the mesmonic flow and go *deeper...*more *primal!*

Uh-oh...

RUUUUMBLE

© Disney

**Early Figment and Dreamfinder character designs
for the Journey Into Imagination ride by X Atencio**

Artwork courtesy of Walt Disney Imagineering Art Collection

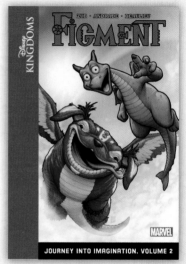